Neighbor Needed 2
David's Song

Teresa Whitaker

Tequan Books

Tequan Books
Brooklyn, New York

ISBN: 978-1-7339148-9-5

First book in this series:

Neighbor Needed
Only the Exceptional Need Apply

For Tequan,
Life is a beautiful song, so play it well.

Table Of Contents

Chapter 1

LAST YEAR

*T*he year after Tasha and Jerome moved to Kew Gardens, I felt the winds of change blow into the Bushwick area of Brooklyn, New York. I guess my small circle of friends was broken. Although I saw Tasha at school often, it was clear the commute from Queens to Brooklyn was taking a toll on her during her first pregnancy. That was when Tasha informed me about her plans to transfer to a school closer to her home in Queens. Since Tasha was the first friend I'd made after moving to Brooklyn, New York from Norfolk, Virginia, I must admit I felt a bit abandoned by my only two close friends. Nevertheless, I, David Reed, was not about to give up on my neighborhood nor on the prospect of finding my forever love.

Sure, Jerome and Tasha would constantly invite me over for dinner, to watch the Super Bowl and to other sporting events at times, but I still didn't want to be the third wheel. At other times, there would be a female friend also invited on days I was invited. Was this a coincidence? I don't think so. How would you feel being fixed up on a blind date by a woman who was once the woman of your dreams? See, Tasha was the total package! She was beautiful, intelligent, caring, and interesting. She was fun to be around, and she was a child magnet. I knew she'd be an awesome mother, because she was a terrific teacher and a wonderful friend. If only Jerome had turned out to be the jerk, I thought he was... But Jerome was just as nice as Tasha. I guess they were meant for each other. They definitely gave me relationship goals.

Well, I still had my job at the Carver School and a subscription to the local gym to keep me busy during the week. My weekends, however, were spent jogging with the Johnsons or biking alone on the bike trail in Highland Park when the weather permitted. I had explored the neighborhood to the max. It was thriving now more than ever. New businesses, restaurants, and entertainment centers were opening all the time. There was plenty to do, but no one to do it with.

Then the Johnsons started inviting me to church. Tasha and Jerome even offered me to be their first baby's godfather, but I declined. The idea of attending church was not foreign to me. After all, I attended church all the time when I was a child. My parents were faithful parishioners. We were at church every Sunday until that fateful day. I digress. I did miss attending church a little, but I needed some time before taking the big step back through the doors.

I filled my time with music—jazz, to be exact. I'd inherited a collection of vinyl records from an uncle when I turned 18. I was a jazz fan ever since I heard Uncle Obie play John Coltrane on his turntable. I found jazz to be so relaxing and soothing to my spirit, that I sometimes fell asleep listening to it. I actually began playing tenor saxophone in eighth grade. I'd even play sax accompanying my mom singing Christmas songs for the family in our living room on Christmas Eve as a tradition.

My mom was so proud of me. She'd tell everyone she knew, her son was now a saxophone player. She even had a picture of me playing sax as her screen saver. She would make video recordings of me every time I'd play. She wanted me to share my gift with everyone, but I stopped playing after she passed away.

Mom asked the pastor at our church to let me play in the band, but that stint only lasted for a few weeks. The elders of the church complained my playing sounded too jazzy and not at all spiritual. I will admit, I got a little carried away on my solos. However, that's when I felt I was the most comfortable and in the spirit. It was like God was speaking through me and my saxophone.

I still remember the day mom surprised me with my very own saxophone. Previously, I would lug the schools' student saxophone home to practice. This one day, she was wearing the biggest smile ever when I walked into our house.

"I bought you a present," mom stated casually.

"Really!" I replied excitedly, with great anticipation—like a child on Christmas morning.

"Yes, really!" she replied, her smile growing even wider.

Then she presented me with my very own brand-new saxophone. I was so amazed, because I knew we could not afford it. Mom had once mentioned she was looking for a used one, since the new ones were so expensive.

So, there I stood with my very own instrument. I had to try it out. My mom was a captive audience. I know I didn't hit all the right notes that time, but mom was so full of excitement and pride that you would have thought I'd just played in the symphony orchestra at the Met. We smiled and laughed as if we were the only two people in the world.

Yes, Martha Reed was my favorite person in this world.

Chapter 2

DAVID REED

When I was a little kid—around four years—old my parents divorced due to irreconcilable differences, and Mom, who was a teacher, raised me on her own from that point on. My dad came to visit us every blue moon, but we never had time to bond like a father and son should. Dad was a corrections officer and worked a lot of overtime. So, mom always held down the fort.

Life wasn't too bad because I had my mom, my Uncle Obie, and my Aunt Tabitha surrounding me. We were a stable family unit. We went to church on Sundays and ate dinner together after church service. Whenever mom needed a babysitter, Aunt Tabitha was ready and waiting. She was a few years younger than mom. Uncle Obie was the eldest. He was a retired postal worker, because he had been injured at his job. He had a back injury from lifting packages that were too heavy. He was now living off his disability check and lived one house away. My Grandma Mae was my favorite, though.

Grandma Mae had been widowed when she was in her seventies, but she had not given up on life. And she never gave up on mom and me. Whenever mom couldn't pick me up from school, Grandma Mae was always there to help. She spoiled me to no end. She also made the best turkey wings, fried chicken, and sweet potato pies. She helped build my confidence and independence after mom passed away.

All of my family members contributed to my receiving a full scholarship to Virginia State University. I spent four years there on a basketball scholarship. My prowess at basketball and my mother's savvy at teaching influenced my decision to become a physical education teacher. After Aunt Tabitha moved to New York, on the year I graduated college, I made my decision to relocate to New York as well after completing my master's degree.

Aunt Tabby, as I lovingly called her, found me both an apartment and a job in my now not-so-new neighborhood. We live together in a huge, antique brownstone on Bushwick Avenue. I live on the third floor in a studio apartment. Tabitha and her fiancé live on the second floor and the landlord, Mr. Gaston, lives on the first floor. Tabitha assured the landlord that I would shovel snow in the winter for him, since he was getting too old for these type of household chores himself. I felt it was a small price to pay for reduced rent and a location just down the street from my job. After all, the rental prices were soaring in the neighborhood due to gentrification. Most minorities could no longer afford to live there if they weren't original homeowners with tenants.

So, here I sit in Brooklyn on a Saturday night alone thinking about my future. I'm listening to a Miles Davis joint tonight. My lesson planning is done. My stomach is full and

I'm not going to intrude on Aunt Tabby and Jordan tonight for mere conversation.

Tonight, my thoughts turn to God and all the lessons my mom taught me before she left. She would always have Bible study, prayer, and praise by herself in the morning. She said spending time with God was the ultimate source of her strength and I saw that demonstrated throughout her life. I didn't even know my mom was sick until she decided to shave all her hair off. She made it seem like a bad perm had caused all her thick, black, long beautiful hair to begin falling out. She said she was going to just shave it all off and start all over again with her hair like when she was a baby. And she looked so beautiful bald head and all. I only began to question her when the hair didn't grow back. I was only sixteen when she told me tearfully that she'd be going home soon. I was confused because we were at home when she told me. Then she explained that there is a home much more beautiful and more important than this one. Then I understood how seriously ill she was. That was when I began to question God.

"How can you take my mother away from me?

How am I supposed to live without her?

Why God? Why?"

Now you know why I don't attend church anymore. I still believe, but I miss my mom. And when she was at her weakest moment all she wanted was for me to play my sax with the church choir, but the pastor would not allow it. So, I played for my mother at home. I played, "A Building not Made by Hand." I played, "His Eye is on the Sparrow." And I played, "I'm Going Up Yonder." She was so happy! Tears of joy rolled down her beautiful face. I wept that night like a baby, but I also made her promises that night. I promised I'd meet her again one day. So, I have to make it there. I also promised to be a force of good in this world and a good father one day. I promised I would forgive my father, too.

My mother passed away that night peacefully in her sleep. She never saw me graduate from high school, college, nor grad school. But I guess she did, right? She saw me do these things from heaven; I say through tears every time I think of her passing. She taught me so much. She taught me how to be a man. She taught me how to treat and respect women. She taught me the importance of getting a good education. She also taught me to forgive. She forgave my dad and she helped me to forgive him, too.

All of my family members could see why I was interested in Tasha. Tasha Clarkson was so much like my mother. She was a strong, independent, black women, and she and her family were church going people. Why wasn't Tasha interested in me? My mother would have been so proud if Tasha could have been her daughter-in -law. But as the Bible says, "All things work together for good..." Although I miss my mom tremendously, I carry her and the lessons she taught me every day in my heart.

Chapter 3

ASIA'S DELIMA

*E*very morning, on my way out of the building I seem to run into my neighbor, Asia. She lives with her grandmother in the building next door. She looks like a runway model every time she walks out of her house. Light, bright and almost white, with long eyelashes, red lipstick, and multicolored eyeshadow, Asia is always ready for her close up. Her clothing is fitted so tightly it looks like she had to oil her skin to slide into them. She wears only stilettos unless it's snowing outside. She smells like a rose in the midst of weeds. Her hair flows like a wavy river down her back beckoning to all men's animal instinct to touch and run their fingers through it. Yeah. I look every day. Hey, I'm a man, aren't I?

But Asia is not the type of woman I'm looking for. She is beautiful, but jaded. She lacks substance and only seems to care about material things. Her shoes Louboutin, her jewelry Tiffany-all of her possessions have high-priced designer names attached to them. I couldn't afford her if I wanted to. Yet, she beckons me each day flirtatiously.

This morning she's wearing a skin-tight red mini dress with white pumps and a matching clutch purse. She shimmies passed me whispering, "Good morning teacher." She winks at me as if to tease me into whispering back. Instead, I say a quick hi and keep on walking. I'm headed to school and I'm not going to be late. The supervisor has been watching me like a hawk lately at school. So, Asia will not distract me today.

As I walk quickly down the avenue, I wonder what Asia will be like ten to twenty years from now. Will her perspective on life ever change? She doesn't have a job. I guess she'll have to eventually sell all her stuff on eBay. Right now, she's dating the owner of a nightclub on Myrtle Avenue. Last month, she was seeing a realtor. I guess Asia was not unable to obtain an apartment of her own as a gift, because that relationship ended too quickly. I'll bet she met the club owner through the realtor, because the jazz club only recently opened. Would Asia stop at this level in her dating game, or would she keep on climbing the social and financial ladder to the billion-dollar club? Women like Asia make me dizzy. She is too much drama for me on any day of the week.

Arriving at the Carver School sobers me from the mesmerizing moment with Asia. My job sharpens my focus. I actually enjoy my job. The children love gym class and I love teaching them how to be healthy for life. After moving my timecard, I race to the gymnasium to begin sorting out the supplies for today's lessons. As soon as I finished, Ms. Adams walks in.

"Good morning," I say energetically.

"Good morning," Ms. Adams replies rigidly.

"How are things going with your classes, Mr. Reed?"

"Very well, Ms. Adams!"

"Do you need any extra equipment?"

"Not at all, but thanks for asking."

"Okay, enjoy your day then."

"Thanks, and same to you."

Ms. Adams always made me feel like I was a part of the team, although I was the newest hire. She was very easy to talk to. I could create events for the children, and she was always willing to hear me out and ultimately assist and accommodate me. She was my dream boss. According to Aunt Tabby, Principal Adams probably had a crush on me. I of course disagreed with that observation. She was a beautiful, educated, and articulate woman, but she seemed a little too sophisticated for my taste. I could not envision her ever wearing sweats or jeans. Besides dating my boss was out of the question.

My days at Carver were slow and easy. Preparing for each class was a rote routine by now. Lunch was the only chance to mingle and enjoy a brief conversation with colleagues. Richard Evans, the math teacher, and Noah Goldberg, the Science teacher, always talked sports with me and challenged me to one-on-one basketball games on weekends. Neither had ever beaten me yet. But it was nice to have some guys to hang out with on some weekends. With Noah now being a newlywed he's not always able to make it to the court. However, he makes up for it by inviting us single guys to his house for dinner every now and then.

Today Noah asked us to meet at the new club that had recently opened up on Myrtle Ave. Richard and I immediately accepted, not having anything else to do on Friday night. We decided to meet at the Blue Angel by 7 pm this Friday with dates, if possible, Noah suggested. His wife, Cindy, was tired of being the only woman at our table while we talked sports. So, Richie and I said we'd try to comply. Then the bell rang, and we all scurried to our classrooms.

My next class was Tasha's class. They were raring and ready to go. Tasha's baby bump looked like a supersized watermelon just about to explode. She was in her seventh month now and I doubted she'd make another month at the job. We chatted briefly then she waddled away slowly. There goes my dream of a future with a family, I think.

The class was so exciting I soon forgot about my broken heart. We played volleyball and started our wind down exercises just before groups of three went to the water fountain for a refreshing drink of water. Everyone was cool, calm, and collected when Tasha walked in to pick up her class. She came right up to me and whispered in my ear, "Can we expect you again for dinner this Friday night?"

"I don't think so. I'm meeting Richard and Noah at the club Friday night, but thanks for the invite."

"Tell Jerome hi for me."

"Will do," Tasha stated before turning to lead her students back to class.

My last class was a bit more challenging in terms of behavior, but once the game started, they put all their energy into competing. Both teams were rewarded, but the best-behaved students earned extra stickers. After putting away the supplies and locking up my office, I punched my timecard and headed home to my empty studio apartment. Two successful years at the Carver School were nearly complete. Settling into the new neighborhood was easy with my Aunt Tabitha and my soon to be Uncle, Jordan, living in the same building. But something was missing.

Chapter 4

BIKE RIDE

*T*omorrow was Friday and I'd get to hang out with Richard, Noah, and Cindy. But tonight, Thursday night, I had no real plans. After some lesson planning, I decided to go for a bike ride up to Highland Park. It was amazing how quickly the Bushwick neighborhood in Brooklyn was changing. You rarely passed African Americans or Hispanics on the streets now. The rent for even studio apartments were way too high for families to stay after many Hasidic Jews purchased and remodeled most of the apartment houses in the area.

There were restaurants and small businesses popping up everywhere. I no longer had to leave the neighborhood to find certain necessary items, services, nor bargains. Fresh organic vegetables were sold at a neighborhood vegetable stand. Vegan restaurants competed with steakhouses for customers. The NYPD patrolled the area constantly to keep the area safe. The crime rate was low, and the children played safely outside their homes. I wondered why Tasha decided to sell the house and move to Queens. *I bet she regrets it now,* I thought as continued biking slowly down the recently created bike lanes.

As I biked, I thought about all the minorities who had been displaced because of gentrification. I felt so badly for them. Where had they gone? Maybe they were being bounced around from shelter to shelter. Some may have even had to change states. There's got to be a better way to deal with the housing crisis in New York. Even Asia and her grandmother were struggling to pay their rent. I guess that's why Asia had to be a gold digger in the first place.

Asia is nice enough. She's a tad flirtatious, but friendly to a fault. She's always inviting me to the club where her boyfriend works. Asia says the Blue Angel is the talk of the town. I bet she'll be surprised to see me there on Friday. That's my surprise. I cannot wait to see her face when I walk in.

My other thoughts will have to wait, because I'm both hungry and thirsty after the long ride on the bike trail. I'm on my way back to eat a nice southern meal at Aunt Tabby's house. I may never learn to cook at this rate.

Chapter 5

AUNT TABBY

I collapsed my foldable bike and jumped into the shower after arriving home from my long ride in the park. As the water rained down my back, I felt such a sense of peace, clarity, and relaxation. After showering, I threw on a pair of my favorite lounging clothes and ran downstairs to my Aunt Tabby's house. I was ravenous.

As usual she greeted me with a huge smile, a tight hug, and a kiss on the face. Then she told me how good I smelled. I thanked her for the compliment and told her I was fresh out of the shower. She replied, "Thank God!" I guess she was remembering those days not so many years ago when I had just come home from basketball practice sweaty and as smelly as dirty clothes inside a hamper for a month.

I laughed and headed to the bathroom to wash my hands before sitting down to the dinner table. By now it was 6 o'clock and soon to be Uncle Jordan had just come in from work. He greeted us both and rushed to put down his briefcase to wash his hands before sitting down to join us at the dinner table.

Aunt Tabby's fried chicken was the closest thing to my mom and grandma's cooking I had tasted in a few weeks. Just one bite transported me back to North Carolina and my childhood. All those happy times around the table came rushing back to mind triggered by the smell of the food, the sound of Aunt Tabitha's voice, and the expressions on her face as we talked. Only Jordan's. Voice pulled me out of the past and back to the reality of the present.

"So, how are things going at the school?"

"Pretty good so far", I replied. I can't complain."

"How's Tasha?"

"About to pop any day now..."

I did not want to tell him I was chosen to host her surprise baby shower but declined due to my former infatuation with her. So, I decided to shift the focus to Aunt Tabby.

"How are things at your school, Aunt Tabby?"

"It's busy as usual. Students are coming in with boo-boos from gym class and recess almost daily. I clean the wounds, bandage them up, and send them back to class after a pep talk about being more careful. A talk that goes in one ear and out of the other on most occasions."

"So, how's the wedding planning coming?"

"It's coming along just fine. I just have to choose a reception venue."

"What about the Blue Angel?"

"I never thought about it, because it's a club."

"Why don't you ask Asia if they would do a wedding reception?"

"I don't know. What do you think, honey?"

"I want what you want. Whatever makes my bride to be happy is fine with me." Uncle Jordan replied.

"Okay then, I'll ask her. It's a black owned business and it's not far from the church."

After that semi-decision, we focused on finishing up our delicious dinner. I cleaned my plate first. Then I offered to take the leftovers home for lunch tomorrow. Of course, Aunt Tabby's reply was yes.

Aunt Tabby treated me like I was her own child since my mom, her sister, passed away when I was a teen. Tabitha was never able to have children and now she was 40 and felt she was too old to conceive a child of her own. Whenever she managed to get into a long-term relationship, that fact always became an issue for the men she dated. Meeting Jordan changed all that. It seems he was a late bloomer who had never settled down with any of his former shallow prospects.

Jordan was only one year older than my aunt Tabitha and he treated her so well.

Jordan was a realtor whose business was thriving, and he was planning to soon purchase a home for the two after their wedding ceremony. Jordan met Tabitha a few years ago while she was looking for an apartment closer to her job site. He'd rented her her first studio apartment in Bedford Stuyvesant only three years ago. After the sale of the apartment, he took a chance and invited her on a date. The rest is history. With rent increases soaring in New York, they made a decision to move in together two years ago after Jordan proposed to Aunt Tabby. For three years, she's been raving to me about what a wonderful man he is. I never get tired of hearing that and I'm just happy to see her smile.

After dinner, we all sat down in the living room and discussed the local news for about an hour before I left to go and do a bit of lesson planning for the next day. Friday, I sighed as I walked towards my apartment. I was surely looking forward to the night out with the fellas. This was my chance to unwind after my weird encounters with Ms. Simpson at the Carver School.

Chapter 6

CARVER SCHOOL

As I walked into the building, I could hear Principal Adams making an announcement. "Will the Sunshine Committee members please report to the conference room immediately. Thanks." I was so thankful that I was not on that committee. See I was more than half an hour early today. This gave me time to set up all the equipment in the gym for each of my classes today. Doing this each morning made for and easy transition from class to class. After setting up the nets for volleyball on one side of the gym, I quickly rolled out a basketball rack to the other side of the gym. As I was placing the cones at one corner of the room Ms. Simpson walked in. That is when I began to hold my breath.

You see, Ms. Simpson was my immediate supervisor and not at all as nice as Ms. Adams. I cringed every time I saw Ms. Simpson at school. She was very condescending and rude to anyone who held a position beneath her. I was surprised she even spoke to me at all, since I was one of the most recent hires at the Carver School. However, I guess new blood is always appealing to vampires. Just a short conversation with her could drain all the optimism out of your body.

"Good morning Mr. Reed. How are you today?"

"I'm doing well. Thanks, Miss Simpson," I replied, while continuing to place the brightly colored cones in the play area for the kindergarteners.

"So, how's life in Bushwick, Mr. Man?"

"I love life in Bushwick, and my name is Mr. Reed."

"In that case, I'll be observing you first period today. Or we could just have a cup of coffee together in the teachers' lounge before class begins."

"Sorry but I've already had breakfast and coffee at home this morning. So, I guess I'll see you the first period."

After hearing my response, Ms. Simpson just rolled her eyes and stomped out of the gymnasium. Then I breathed a sigh of relief.

At that moment Richard and Noah poked their heads in to remind me to meet them at the club at 7:00 PM.

"I'll be there on time. Make sure you two get there on time!"

"See you there!" they yelled back.

The first period observation by Ms. Simpson seemed to last a decade. The kindergarten children seemed puzzled that she was watching their every move. One of them even said, "What is she doing here, Mr. Reed?" I told little Nicholas she wants to see you guys play the game and he said, "Oh, does she want to play too?" Could you imagine Ms. Simpson in her high heels and mini skirted suit bending down and stooping to the level of kindergarten children to play a physical game in the gymnasium? That would never happen. She was only there to see me sweat and she waited for as long as she could for that little bit of perspiration that never came. The children were so well behaved and thoroughly enjoyed playing their little relay races and the Steal the Bacon game. So, she could say nothing to belittle me in her observation notes. What she didn't know or couldn't see was this was not just a job to me; it was my joy.

Periods two through eight breezed by. As I was moving my timecard from the in slot to the out slot, I heard a voice over my shoulder beckoning me to meet in Ms. Simpson's office. It was the voice of the school secretary. So, I placed my card back into the in slot and walked a few steps across the hall into the "devil's den" which is what I call Ms. Simpson's office. There she was sitting in her office chair at her desk with her legs crossed holding my observation report in her hands. She was like a hawk camouflaged on a tree's limb awaiting a chance to swoop down on its prey.

Ms. Simpson greeted me quickly and began to rave about my performance as a teacher. She then stated I had a beautiful rapport with my students, and she could tell how much the kindergarteners adored me.

"Would you like to have children one day Mr. Reed," Ms. Simpson said excitedly while grinning widely.

"Maybe someday, with the right person, I would like to have children."

"Maybe the right person is right in front of you. Who knows?"

After that weird and uncomfortable statement, Ms. Simpson began pointing out my flaws during today's lesson. She felt I could have done better lesson planning, although she had never seen nor asked for my lesson plan. Ms. Simpson actually believed these kindergarten children should have been able to state what they learned from the gym class lesson that day. I just nodded okay and told her I had to be somewhere soon. So, she handed me the observation report. I signed it, thanked her for the advice, and left her office as quickly as I could.

Chapter 7

BLUE ANGEL

I arrived at the Blue Angel Jazz Club at 6:45 PM. The lighting was calm and relaxing. The music floated on the air like fluffy clouds in a blue sky. I needed this... a night out on the town with no worries. This was a chance to be carefree and just have a good time talking with friends. Richard and Noah were going to be late as usual. So, I decided to order myself a non-alcoholic drink. I ordered a virgin pina colada drink. Just as I was about to sip my drink guess who comes walking over to my table? Asia. Asia came sashaying over to my table offering to sit down and keep me company. I accepted her offer while nervously glancing around and hoping the owner of the club, her boyfriend, would not see us sitting together. I did not want to cause a scene and ruin my night out with the boys.

So, Asia sat there across from me in this beautiful skintight fuchsia colored mini dress, a V-neck sinking almost to her navel, crystal or diamond earrings dangling from her ears like bulbs on a Christmas tree and clear stiletto shoes that showed her beautiful pink and white perfectly manicured toes. What man could resist this temptress? Delilah in the Bible had nothing on Asia. I was beginning to perspire just from sitting across the table. Her perfume was sweet smelling and as alluring as her attire. Her red lips were as enticing as a strawberry atop a slice of shortcake. I was lost in her light brown eyes as she spoke to me in a near whisper.

"So, David, how do you like it?"

"Like what?"

"How do you like the club, teacher? I never thought I'd see you here."

"I wanted you to be surprised, Asia."

"Well, I am truly surprised by your visit, David. Are you meeting someone?"

"I'm just hanging out with some of the guys from work tonight."

"Oh, I thought you were meeting a date."

"No, not tonight, but maybe in the near future."

"Well, she'll be a very lucky girl."

"Thanks, neighbor."

"Well, I have to go now, I see Marcus has just arrived. He'll want me to help him greet people."

"Okay, later!"

The dimly lit club put me in a tranquil mood. The live music is superb. Asia was right, this is the place to be on a Friday night. Everyone is dressed from casual to dressy, some in suit jackets and some in dress shirts. The menu is also inviting. There is even a vegan section on the menu. Then I notice there are no alcoholic beverages listed. This is a safe and decent venue. I'll be sure to tell Aunt Tabby and Jordan about these aspects of the Blue Angel Jazz Club.

It's now approaching seven thirty pm and I'm getting hungry. I motion to the waitress for service and am about to make my order when Noah, Cindy, and Richard waltz in.

"Wait one minute," Richard says. I can't believe you were about to eat without us."

"That's why friends should be more prompt when meeting friends for a night out on the town."

Everyone sits down after greeting each other. We all order the recommended dish of the evening and Cindy and Noah are disappointed to find there's no wine on the menu.

"Have we been invited to a church?" Noah complains as he opts for cranberry juice.

Cindy quickly and lovingly reprimands him as she comments on how well decorated the club is. We all love the music, the lighting, and the food we've ordered.

Later, our conversation changes to the work week. This is when Noah and Richard inform me of the fact that they overheard Ms.

Simpson talking to me in the gymnasium that morning.

"Why didn't you interrupt the conversation and save me from Ms. Simpson's wrath?" I say as they laugh.

"We wanted to see you squirm," Richard says grinning.

"You should have just agreed to have coffee with her that morning and you wouldn't have had to be observed by her," Noah says adding insult to injury.

"No way! Then she would sink her claws further into my skin every time I see her in the future."

"This is why I hate going out with you guys", Cindy interjects. "I'm tired of hearing about that school and sports. I wish you two would get some female friends for me to bond with. Maybe we could help you guys become more well-rounded."

"We do talk about other things sometimes," I add.

"Like what?" Cindy teases.

"We talk about gentrification and rent hikes in the neighborhood." Richard chimes in.

"Now that's a great topic for discussion!" Cindy adds.

Chapter 8
GENTRIFICATION

So, as you know there is currently a housing crisis in New York. Rent hikes are both expected and common. Low-income housing is scarce, and the minorities are affected the most by this predicament. In addition, we have the advent of minority neighborhoods being gentrified by mostly Caucasians, or Hasidic Jews. So, you know this is a hot topic. Therefore, in my mind I'm thinking, "Let the games begin!"

"I think gentrification is good for Bushwick because we're bringing more businesses into the community." Cindy says.

"What about the small business owners who were already here and are now finding it difficult to survive because gentrifiers are taking their customers and purchasing their buildings and hiking up the rent?" Richard retorts.

"You have to weigh the pros and cons," Noah says taking his position as the peacemaker. "There's a lower crime rate now, too. However, the rent is too high."

Then I begin to relay Asia's dilemma to everyone as Aunt Tabby and Uncle Jordan walk in and invite themselves to our table. They ask for two extra chairs placed next to me. They quickly place an order and join the conversation.

"Asia and her grandmother's situation can be filed under the rent-controlled apartments versus the cost of living going up for landlord's part of this argument. I add. Their landlord says he's no longer making a profit on his rent-controlled properties. In fact, he's going into the red due to all the maintenance he has to do on each building. Besides, he has his own mortgage and other bills to pay. If this problem continues, Asia's landlord will sell the building and the tenants will be homeless."

"Yes, I know at my school there's a large influx of students who live in homeless shelters." Aunt Tabby chimes in.

"And I'm showing properties from foreclosures and apartment buildings like Asia's daily." Uncle Jordan concurs.

In the back of my mind, I'm wondering if Aunt Tabby and Uncle Jordan know that our own landlord is being approached daily by Hasidic Jews who are offering to buy his house in cash. Yet I'm glad my uncle and aunt are about to purchase their own home, so we won't be added to the growing list of homeless minorities in Bushwick.

"This is not just a financial issue. This is a racial issue, too." Richard says interrupting my thoughts. "When certain types of people want an area, they use their financial power to get it."

"So, are you saying these other races of people are running minorities out of Bushwick?" Noah interjects.

"What he is saying is that in the past two years we're seeing less people who look like us and more people who look like you in this area." I reply.

"However, you are seeing more businesses open and that gives people in the community more job opportunities." Cindy says.

Then, I think of the five new restaurants and the television studio that have opened in less than a two-block radius of my apartment building and think how wonderful that is for those who can afford it. Those businesses were created for the newcomers, not for those who already lived here.

"I disagree, because those businesses bring their own employees with them." Richard states. "The only job opportunities created are those of babysitting children, parking cars for the celebrities and executives at the television studio and cleaning the newer residents' homes."

"So, what can we do to make things better in our community?" Noah asks.

"Maybe we can join in with tenants like Asia and rally up some support for them. This way the entire culture of the community won't be lost, and we can move more towards the beautiful mosaic Martin Luther King Jr dreamt of." I state.

"Then let's do it!" Noah yells.

"Okay. Now, can we talk about a lighter topic, guys?" Cindy asks.

"Yes. I want to talk about renting this beautiful venue for my wedding reception." Aunt Tabby pleasantly interjects.

On that note all conversation changes to butterflies, roses, and romance and I'm a little relieved.

Chapter 9

WEDDING PLAN

A unt Tabby is right. The ambience of the Blue Angel would be perfect for a wedding reception. Tonight's décor is a vibe. Light blue lighting, flickering faux candles at the center of each of the guests' tables, and crystal chandeliers set the chill mood. An intimate medium sized stage allows for a piano, a drum set, a guitar stand, a bass guitar stand, trumpet, and saxophone players to serve as a small band to accompany singers. That's for those who want live music. In the opposite corner sits a fully equipped DJ booth for those who just want to play and mix recordings. Besides, the club could easily seat 250 people.

"Hey Marcus!" I yell as he's about to pass by our table.

"Let me introduce you to my Aunt Tabby."

"Hello," Aunt Tabby says as quickly as she can.

She doesn't want to miss this opportunity to book the Blue Angel. Suddenly, Asia sashays over to our table after greeting some other guests she's seated close by. After overhearing Tabby's plans, Asia offers to help decorate and plan the reception. When Aunt Tabby states she wants me to play Stevie Wonders a "Ribbon in the Sky" on sax, Marcus takes note and asks if I'd like to play something tonight. I reply no immediately. The wedding is two months away in July and I'm a bit rusty. I need these two months to practice.

Marcus agrees to the date and the rest of the night we all eat, chat, and enjoy the music. That is until Noah and Richard remind me the surprise baby shower is on this Monday. Tabby looks me straight in the eye feeling my pain of losing the girl of my dreams to Jerome Johnson as well as her own pain of not being able to produce a child. We both suck it up, as everyone starts suggesting ideas for baby gifts. Cindy, Asia, and Tabby create their own group conversation while looking at Tasha and Jerome's baby shower registry on their phones.

I tell Noah I'll order something from their registry tomorrow. Then I ask why they changed the date. Richard explains Tasha had been feeling a little more exhausted than usual this week and might start her leave earlier than expected.

"She looked like she was ready to pop that baby out today." Noah interjected.

"Her stomach is huge!" I add.

"I guess after the baby is born Tasha will leave her position at Carver for good and begin working at her new school in Kew Gardens." Richard chimed in.

"So, I guess she's the one who got away, huh?" Noah asks me.

"No need to cry over spilled milk." I retort as I get up to go to the men's room.

On my way there I hear the voice of an angel emanating through the club. This voice is light, mellow, yet sultry. So, I turn my attention to the stage. And there she stands in a floor length yellow sequined gown, her boxed braided hair is adorned with gold ornaments and pulled up into a neat bun. Her low heeled, gold-colored with straps around the ankle shoes top off her look. Ms. Lauren Wilson's caramel colored skin is wrapped in gold and yellow hues like a butter scotch candy. Her red lip stick shines as her lips drip words of the song on the microphone. She's classy, yet sassy. And I like everything I see and hear. Lauren is singing, Billie Holiday's, "Them There Eyes." Suddenly, I don't have to go anymore. I'm mesmerized by the sight and the sound of this lovely lady. Time stands still as she finishes each note. My heart starts to beat again as the song finishes. As she exits the stage to applause, I feel I must meet her. This is my one chance and I have to make it happen.

As I start to approach Lauren, a much older man walks up to her, kisses her on the jaw, and presents her with a bouquet of flowers. So, I stand there frozen in place, but I notice she wears no wedding band on her left ring finger. I begin to breathe again as I make my way to the men's room. As I wash my hands at the sink, the older gentleman enters the room. I say to him, "What a performance!" His response frees me.

"Yes, my daughter is very talented!"

"Congratulations!"

"Thanks, young man. You'd better hurry up, she's about to sing again."

"Okay! Bye then." I say as I rush back to my seat.

Marcus is still at the table, so I tell him I may be interested in playing saxophone on a Friday night in the near future.

"Why the sudden change of heart, David?"

"Um, I just realized the caliber of talent you hire here is all."

"Oh, you mean you noticed Lauren."

"No. I mean yeah. You know what I mean."

"Well, let me just warn you that she is a Christian and I don't think she's looking for a relationship right now."

"And how would you know that?"

"She talks to Asia all the time about how she's completing her master's degree in hopes of teaching music in an elementary school."

"Well, I work in an elementary school. So, we have something in common."

"Well, just remember you've been warned."

"Thanks, man."

Everyone at our table notices how quiet and focused I am all of a sudden. I don't care because I'm enjoying Lauren's set. As soon as she finishes, I'm going to introduce myself to her. Or maybe I should just have Asia introduce me. No, that's not going to work. I've changed my mind altogether now and I'm ready to leave.

NEIGHBOR NEEDED 2: DAVID'S SONG

"Why am I so nervous?" I think to myself.

Then I tell everyone it's been a long night and I'm about to go home. Everyone agrees to end our night out. We pay our bills and leave huge tips. As I exit the building, I overhear Lauren talking to a fan.

"You can hear me sing tomorrow at First Baptist Church." she says as I keep walking towards Jordan and Aunt Tabby's car.

Another opportunity missed since I am not going to church anytime soon.

Chapter 10
TASHA

*T*he weekend breezes by and here I am again back on the hamster's wheel at the Carver School. The day begins and ends on good notes. Then I hear the magic words, Mrs. Johnson please report to the library to pick up your report card envelopes after dismissal. This is code for the surprise baby shower is about to begin. I race to the library to hide in the darkened room with all the colleagues who have eighth period preparation periods.

After about fifteen minutes we hear footsteps. Then the door opens, and we all scream, "Surprise!"

"Oh, my goodness! You guys almost caused my water to break!"

Everyone gathers around her to give Tasha their own special greeting and individual hug. I'm the last one in line. When I finish my embrace, Tasha says, "You're really good at keeping secrets, David."

"Only those that involve you." I respond as she raises her brows.

At that exact moment, Jerome walks in.

"Surprise, honey!"

"So, you were in on this, too!"

"Guilty as charged."

Then, the music and games begin. The catered food is extravagant and filling. There's chicken, rice and beans, a variety of salads, fruit, fish, vegetarian dishes, and even ribs. Noah, Richard, and I sit together and chat as we chow down.

Tasha decides to cut the huge cake shaped like a baby carriage before opening a few of her gifts that were brought to the school. All other registry gifts were going to arrive at her home in the next few days. After cutting the cake she and Jerome feed each other their slices like they did with their wedding cake at their nuptials. I feel sick to my stomach, but I grin and bear it as always. Then Tasha sits in her special chair, wearing her special baby shower hat, and begins opening gifts. By the time she gets to the third gift, she winces a little. Jerome looks concerned, but Tasha says, "It's nothing. I've just been on my feet too long today."

As Tasha continues to open gifts, I spot a puddle of water starting to form on the floor in front of her. Suddenly, Tasha starts to scream, "The baby is coming!" Everyone scrambles to get help. The paramedics arrive and rush Tasha and Jerome to the nearest hospital.

News spreads on Tuesday throughout the school about Tasha having been in labor for nearly 24 hours and having finally given birth to a baby boy. The name is... You guessed it: Jerome Johnson Junior. Everyone's happy for the couple and anxiously awaiting the first picture of their bundle of joy. Noah, Richard, and I plan to go visit Tasha and her baby at Wycoff Hospital after work today. I'm a little reluctant to join them, but I feel I must go out of loyalty to Tasha as a friend and colleague.

Our crew is the first wave of visitors at the hospital. We rush to see the baby behind the glass first. The guys and I agree the baby looks like his father. Only I notice, Junior has his mother's nose. Noah and Richard feel only I would notice that.

Once inside Tasha's hospital room, the conversation changes. We all arrange our floral presents on her nightstand and read our cards to her as she smiles with her motherly glow. Tasha jokes about her baby boy having the three of us as uncles teaching him how to play basketball. When the guys leave Tasha and I alone in the room, I tell Tasha her baby is so beautiful, and he could have been ours. She looks a little uncomfortable when I say this, but grins back at me in a friendly way. On that note, I say my goodbyes and wish her all the best as a new mother. Her final words to me are: "Don't be a stranger." With that thought, I walk out of her room to join Noah and Richard on a ride back to our neighborhood.

Back in my apartment, I ponder thoughts of what could have been between Tasha and me dissolve, as opposed to the possibilities for Lauren and me if I make an effort to meet her. I fall asleep dreaming of Lauren singing songs to only me.

Chapter 11

RENT

Wednesday morning, I see Asia as I walk out of my building, but Asia is not her usual cheerful and flirtatious self. She looks worried.

"Is everything okay?" I ask as I approach her.

"Not really, our landlord has decided to sell the building and my grandmother, and I cannot afford the rental prices other apartment building landlords are asking for. So, I'm afraid we may have to move into a homeless shelter soon."

"Can't you get an extra job to help with the rent, Asia?"

"I don't qualify for any high paying jobs because I dropped out of school when I was 17 to help care for my mother. After my mother passed away, I continued to live with my grandmother. See my mother battled drug addiction for years and at the end of her life my grandmother let us live with her. Why do you think I date all these guys? They give me money and I use that money to make ends meet. I'm ashamed to admit it, but it's the truth, David."

"So, go back to school! There are lots of GED programs in our neighborhood."

"You're right. I should go back to school, but that will take time and I don't have time right now."

"Well, I'm going to inquire with the principal to find a GED program close to home for you in the meantime."

"Thanks, teacher!"

"Talk to you later, Asia."

I rush off to work trying not to be late. I feel so badly for Asia and her grandmother that I keep thinking of ways to solve their problem throughout the day. Once I finally speak with the principal about a cite that prepares people for the GED exam, I start to feel a little better. I keep hearing my mom quoting the Bible and saying, "Love thy neighbor as thy self." My mother would be so proud of me for what I'm doing for Asia.

Then a new thought pops into my mind. Maybe Noah, Richard, and I could organize a rally to fight for rent control or at least make new landlords aware of families like Asia's. So, I'll wait for Noah and Richard in the parking lot after school to discuss some of my ideas.

After a brief discussion we agree to meet with likeminded neighbors this Friday night at the Blue Angel. Noah suggests we get Cindy involved since she works at City Hall. I intend to coax Aunt Tabby and Jordan into our group since Jordan is a real estate agent. Richard believes Marcus will want to be involved due to his current relationship status with Asia. However, we all wonder how we're going to pull this off being teachers when tomorrow is June first, and we have tons of paperwork to do.

As soon as I get home, I wash up and run downstairs to Aunt Tabby's house. When Jordan enters both Aunt Tabby and I are ready to pounce on him and convince him to join our cause. To our surprise he is reluctant to join because his bosses don't want him to abate home buyers in the area. I see his point and I don't want to cause problems in their relationship. So, I change the subject and eat dinner quietly before taking my leave. Aunt Tabby whispers quietly at the door, "Don't worry, David. I'll be there on Friday night." I kiss her and say goodnight.

Once inside of my upstairs apartment, I complete all my students' report card grades and comments before going to bed.

Chapter 12

COMMUNITY MEETING

*T*hursday blurs into Friday morning when I catch Asia stepping out of her gate in a blue polka dot dress and white stilettos. I race to give her the information about the GED program starting next week only a block away at the community center. She takes the paperwork as I tell her about our rally plans. I think I see a tear fall from Asia's eye as she thanks me and hurries off to Marcus' car waiting down the street.

When I get to school, Richard hands me fifty flyers to hand out to parents after school. He says in a whisper, "We don't want to get into trouble for handing them out to the children at school. You know Ms. Simpson is always looking to start trouble and to usurp her authority over all the teaching staff." I concur and speed off to pick up my first period class.

"Going into politics, are we?" I hear Ms. Simpson say as my class and I start the warmup routine.

I notice she has a flyer in her hand as she approaches me. I motion to one of my grade four students to take over and lead the class in warming up. Shawn takes over and I try to put out the flames of Ms. Simpson's evil devices before it spreads to the principal and jeopardizes our jobs. I'm praying under my breath that Jesus will help me.

"I found the original copy of your groups' flyer under the cover of the copy machine in the main office. You know that is against the school's rules, Mr. Reed."

"I'm glad you found it, Ms. Simpson because I was going to invite you to the meeting tonight at the Blue Angel."

"I'm flattered, David. However, I won't be able to make it since my PHD class meets tonight."

"That's too bad. I was looking forward to seeing you there."

"Don't worry we can meet there on some other evening when there's just the two of us."

I try to smile as I agree to her invitation. I know that disagreeing with her could cause Richard, Noah, and I to be called into a disciplinary meeting, so I pretend to be interested in her just this one time.

"Okay, David, enjoy your day and your night!" Ms. Simpson says as she exits the gym.

"Whew! That was a close call." I say to myself as I resume my role as teacher.

The day became much easier after that close encounter. I gave each class free time after attendance and warmups for the remainder of the day. Then at days end I gave out flyers, rushed home, changed clothes, and headed to our planning meeting at the Blue Angel.

Marcus was quite happy with the number of people we brought in. He provided free lemonade for all attendees. Of course, he viewed them all as possible new customers. There were at least a hundred people in attendance. Unfortunately, Marcus had given Lauren the night off. I was hoping to introduce myself to her tonight. Instead, I'd be able to give my undivided attention to the cause at hand.

The actual meeting started at 4:30 pm. Noah took the stage first to welcome our guests. Richard detailed our plan to get our petition signed so that Cindy could have it reach the mayor's office. I summed everything up by detailing exactly what we wanted: low-income housing, rent control, or stipends to assist tenants who just could not make ends meet because of constant rent hikes. We were also requesting more education programs and training for job placement.

The crowd's applause reached a crescendo after my presentation which included a PowerPoint slideshow. As I looked out at the crowd, I noticed Aunt Tabby standing next to Lauren. Yes, Lauren was supporting our cause. This must be a good sign, I thought. Then I decided to add a short yet poignant speech about gentrification in our neighborhood.

"People, it was just two years ago that I relocated to this Bushwick neighborhood in New York from Virginia. However, I was lucky enough to have a job and a low-income apartment waiting for me. My Aunt and her fiancé were already settled here and had arranged for me to have an interview at a school near our apartment building. After landing a job, I found some forever friends in this ever-changing landscape we call our neighborhood.

"When I arrived, Bushwick was already a few years in to being gentrified. It was going from being predominantly Hispanic and African American to being largely Caucasian and Jewish. Hispanics and African American residents were leaving due to homes and apartment buildings being sold to new owners who charged way more for rent. Many of these families were being forced into homelessness and this is why we're here.

"While gentrification has created a more colorful mosaic like community, it has also caused some problems. New businesses and job opportunities are popping up every day. Restaurants with more cultural varieties of food can be found and enjoyed on almost every corner. Entertainment venues and even television studios have shown up in our neighborhood as well. Even the police presence has increased. Can you believe it? This is all good, right?

"However, the fact remains that-people-good people are being displaced. They are not getting these new jobs, and many don't have the education they need to qualify for these new positions. And many of the new businesses bring their workers with them.

"People, this more colorful mosaic can work for all of us. But we must empathize with the least of us if our neighborhood is ever going to truly be great!

"Thank you all for coming out in support of our cause and please sign our petition on your way out."

Again, the crowd roared with applause as people lined up to sign the petition.

Chapter 13

LAUREN

After all the attendees of our meeting cleared out, I go over to thank Aunt Tabby for coming. However, she stops me midway through my sentence and introduces me to Lauren. She's a little shy at first but warms up after a few laughs. Aunt Tabby slyly makes her exit leaving me to walk home by way of Lauren's house. I hate to admit it but I'm so glad she did.

Now I have Lauren entirely to myself. Her deep-set dimples and large brown eyes placed me in a trance. I don't want to wake up from this daydream. Unfortunately, she lives only three blocks away from the Blue Angel. So, I have no choice but to end our conversation more abruptly than I want to.

"Can I get your number, Lauren? I'd really like to carry this conversation further."

"Sure, David. I'll await your call."

"So, what are you doing tomorrow?"

"Nothing but my usual weekend chores around the house. Why do you ask?"

"I wanted to ask you out to lunch."

"I'll go out to lunch with you tomorrow, if you promise to go to church with me on Sunday."

I want to decline the offer to go to church, but I don't want to miss a chance to see Lauren again. So, I agree to go to church this Sunday. We say our goodbyes and I bebop down the street with a stride that shows I was able to get Lauren's number. Suddenly, my cell phone rang. So, I stopped to answer it.

"Hi, baby boy!"

"Grandmama Mae! Is that you?"

"Yes, baby it's me. How are you doing?"

"I'm doing well, grandma. "How are you and Uncle Obie doing?"

"We're doing well and we're looking forward to coming up there for Tabitha's wedding."

"I can't wait to see you two."

"We'll be there on June 30th. You know I hate to fly, but I must see my baby girl get married."

"Tabby will be so happy that all of us can be there."

"I hope you have a date for the reception, so you can finally stop pining over that other girl. What's her name again?"

"Her name is Tasha, grandma. You don't have to worry about her anymore. Tasha and her husband recently welcomed their first child. So, I'm completely over her."

"Good! So, get you a date for the wedding."

"I'm working on it."

"Okay, see you soon. Love you."

"Love you, too. Bye."

As I approach my apartment, I sigh, and hope Lauren turns out to be as nice as I expected.

Chapter 14

DATING

As I lie in bed comparing Lauren to Tasha this Saturday morning, I am more relaxed than I've been in weeks. Lauren is more bohemian than Tasha. Lauren wears her hair in natural hair styles, while Tasha perms hers. I also like the way Lauren is active in her community, and not only in her church. We even have a love of music in common. Lauren sings and I play sax. She is just about two years younger than I am, and my mother would say that's a good thing. Mom always said girls mature faster than boys.

However, Lauren is clearly a "daddy's girl" so, I'm hoping that won't be a problem. Her father is definitely her number one fan and our first meeting in the men's room was a bit awkward. He did tell me to rush to see his daughter perform, though. This has me thinking he's looking for a proper suitor for his daughter. This thought jolts me back into reality and I begin to prepare myself for our date.

I planned to take Lauren to brunch at one of my favorite restaurants. I pick her up at 11:00am. She looks amazing in her emerald, green coat and brown Uggs boots. She's very comfortably dressed, and her hair is a bouncing bunch of loose brown spirals. She's smiling widely at me as she descends the staircase of the three-story brownstone building. Nick's Italian Restaurant is only 5 blocks away, but I call a cab because I don't want to appear to be cheap on our first date.

At the restaurant, our conversation is smooth and easy. I feel as though I've known Lauren my whole life. We talked about music, family, work, and our life goals in one sitting. At the end of our meal, I noticed Lauren had some spaghetti sauce on the corner of her mouth. I want to lick it off myself, but I realize that would be an inappropriate action this soon in our relationship. *Still, I can dream, can't I?* I offer Lauren to order dessert, but she declines.

Instead, she says she must go to the powder room to freshen up. My eyes scan her entire body as she stands, turns, and makes her way to the restroom. *Dear Lord, she's wearing that sweater dress,* I think as I try to calm down before the waitress approaches with the bill. The burgundy and brown dress was a total coverup to her neckline but left nothing to imagination in terms of Lauren's soda bottle shaped body. My hands amongst other things were a bit moist as I paid the bill awaiting Lauren's return to the table.

I patted my forehead with a napkin when I saw Lauren approach our table again. "I don't want this date to end," Lauren squeals as she reaches for her coat. "Well, it doesn't have to end just yet." I reply. "Why don't we go for a walk so we can talk some more."

"That would be nice but it's a little chilly out."

"No worries." You can have my scarf and I'll hold your hand to keep you warm."

"Let's take a cab to Highland Park and walk the path. It's beautiful there this time of year."

The park is so picturesque, an autumn dream. We are walking, living postcard. We cuddle and walk together as the wind blows across our faces. I can't help but think back to the day I met Tasha as we walk down the very same path together. Lauren interrupts my DeJa'Vu moment asking what I'm thinking about.

Should I tell her or just change the subject? I really don't know what Lauren would think of me thinking of another woman while on a date with her. Do I lie to her or tell her the truth? I don't want to ruin my chance with Lauren, but the truth is my thoughts of Tasha still haunt me. My flashback is interrupted by Lauren's loving gaze as she pauses and tippy toes to kiss me on the jaw.

"What was that for?" I ask.

"Nothing," she replies as all memories of Tasha fade into the past where they belong.

"So, I'll see you tomorrow at church."

"Yes, definitely!" I reply.

I take Lauren home and give her a peck on the cheek. She smiles shyly and I turn to walk away towards home.

Once inside my building, Aunt Tabby greets me at the door of my apartment.

"So, how did the date go?" She says.

"It went very well and I will be joining Lauren at church tomorrow."

"It must have gone well, if you're willing to attend church."

"I know I have been avoiding church long enough. It's time to deal with my issues and avoid taking the same problems into the future."

"Good for you. I'm so happy for you nephew."

"Okay then, Aunt Tabby go and get some rest."

"Good night, nephew. I love you!"

"Love you, too."

Chapter 15

CHURCH

*I*n the morning, I arose, refreshed with a newer brighter, outlook on life. I was ready for a change, and I was ready to open myself up to love as I prepared for the day. I started singing some old church hymns I remembered from my childhood I made a quick omelette for breakfast and washed it down with a glass of orange juice. I was not about to be late for my date at church with Lauren. I was in a very mellow mood today.

Now, my only problem was what to wear. I could wear a suit, but that was too preacher like for me. I decided to wear a dressy casual look some black chinos, a black turtleneck shirt and a tan cardigan with black laced up shoes. My look would not draw attention to me in the service. I just wanted to stand out enough for Lauren to see me.

As I entered the midsized church, the pastor, Lauren's father was about to be called up to the podium to preach. I quickly and quietly sat down on the end seat in the back of the church. After Lauren's dad greeted everyone, he asked his daughter to come up and sing a solo before his sermon. *Wow!* I thought. *I'm going to get to hear Lauren sing today, too. I am so glad I agreed to come to church.*

Lauren's voice was so angelic, it lifted me out of myself and made me think heavenly thoughts of Jesus. The experience brought back all of my memories of Sundays in church as a little boy with my mother. It was so comforting and moving at the same time. Lauren was singing Amazing Grace.

A tear fell from my left eye as she sang the song and I knew I was in the right place at the right time. Something was healing me and I was finding closure. I was no longer angry with God about my mother's death. I just felt an amazing sense of peace inside. All of this happened before the sermon.

Lauren walked all the way to the back of the church to sit with me on the last pew in the church. She greeted me with a soft kiss on my cheek and a welcoming hug. I could tell she was happy to see me.

When Lauren's father started preaching about forgiveness and I could really relate to all the examples he gave. Remember, I never really forgave my dad for leaving my mother to raise me alone. I even had a grudge against God for my mother's death. So, when Pastor Williams presented the story of ultimate forgiveness and redemption, I could not resist the calling of God on me to forgive. When the alter call was made, I was the first to go up to the front to be prayed for and to make a new commitment to God. Lauren told me before I went forward that I didn't have to do this for her.

I replied, "I'm not doing this for you. I'm doing this for myself. If things don't work out for us, we will just be friends there's no pressure for you to accept me as more than that. Thanks for inviting me here today."

With that being said, Lauren released my hand and let me go to walk into the arms of Jesus. Yes, I gave my heart to God and I no longer felt lonely.

The church workers gave me a Bible and some other a literature before we were dismissed. Then I went home to have dinner with Aunt Tabby. I couldn't wait to tell her the news.

Of course, she was thrilled. She hugged me so tightly, I could barely breathe. I slept like a baby that night.

Chapter 16

OUR COMMUNITY

My week at school started calmly. There were no pop-up observations by the principal and no jokes from the guys about my faith. The students are always my favorite part of the school day anyway, and they are all maturing at the routines now. So it doesn't even feel like I'm working most of the time. Almost every child's favorite class is Jim, right!

By Wednesday, things started happening in the neighborhood though. Asia was having problems again with her landlord. He was raising the rent again now Asia had just started a program to get her GED. Next, she plan to take nursing courses while doing home healthcare for her grandmother if she had to move out, her plans would be delayed indefinitely so the guys and I had to move faster to make an impact with the rally the signatures we acquired at the blue Angel had reached our local officials and they were publicizing our issues. Our congressman and our community leaders were contacting us and we're offering to speak at our rally on behalf of residence like Asia. Now to call another meeting and get the press to attend. Then we were thinking of having a round table, discussion with the landlords tenants and politicians to draw up a list of to - do's to bring about a change to Bushwick's ongoing gentrification problems. Noah, Richard and I plan to discuss this idea at my apartment tonight.

After dinner at my Aunt Tabby's, I met with Noah and Richard to work out all the details of the next rally and the concluding meeting as we talked and divided duties my phone rang. It was Lauren on the phone.

"Hey David, how is it going?"

"It's all good Lauren how are you?"

"I'm fine. My week is going well. I have an interview for a job at school next week."

"Great honey! I hope you get it." I replied.

"I have to go now, though. I'm planning the rent rally with my boys." I continued.

"Can I be of any help?" Lauren asked.

"Well I think we have it all together now."

"Wait a minute! Maybe I could sing at the rally!" Lauren suggested

"I would love that idea. Let's talk later and we can work out the details. "

"Okay. Cool."

My friends and I completed all the rally planning and we all went home to retire for the evening, but not before I told them about my new dating situation and my spiritual transformation. Noah and Richard were quite happy for me. They encouraged me to continue on my path. They even felt I was happier than usual. They were right. The feelings of loneliness were gone, chased away by the presence of God and my budding new relationship with Lauren. It was easy getting to sleep that night.

Chapter 17

RALLY

On Saturday, our crew met at the Blue Angel for a little pep-talk then we loaded all our items for the rally into Richards minivan. We rode in silence for a few minutes. Then we shouted, "Wow!" The park was full to the max. From a distance, we could hear a rumbling of voices in anticipation of our rally. There must've been thousands of people out there. Every local news outlet was covering our event. Cameras and news reporters littered the front of the venue with a mic stand full of news affiliate microphones. We jumped out of Richard's van and set up tables with chairs, flyers, and buttons. We handed out signs, with "The Rent is Too High" and "Save the Poor and Needy" written on them.

Noah spoke to the crowd first as an example of a newcomer to the neighborhood.

He would explain the pros of gentrification to the crowd while Richard, who was next in line to speak, would explain the cons. The crowd was not as understanding of Noah, but they listened anyway. Some of the pros Noah mentioned in his speech were an increase in job opportunity, better schools, safer streets and exposure to different cultures; while Richard talked about cons like, the rent being to high for residents who may have to relocate.

Then Asia came to the podium and spoke on her individual problem. The crowd roared with thunder after her testimonial with chants of "The Rent is Too high!" Finally, Lauren belted out, Marvin Gaye's, "What's Going On." The crowd swayed in unison as she sang the song. The rest of us gave out buttons and flyers.

Then to our surprise, the mayor arrived. He slowly approached the podium and offered a solution for both renters and the landlords. He asked landlords to rethink the amount of their rental hike prices and start lower rather than higher. He acts the landlords to empathize with tenants who make less money, but we're good tenants who pay rent on time. He asked tenants with bad rent paying reputations to improve or risk being evicted. Finally, he posed the solution for the housing crisis. He said all abandoned properties, not sold to buyers at a reasonable price by the fall would be turned into affordable housing by the city. The crowd roared in agreement with the mayor. Stevie Wonder's, "Living for the City" could be heard emanating through air as the crowd dissipated out of the park and into a newly refueled and recharged neighborhood. Our work here was done.

Chapter 18

RELATIONSHIP GOALS

*L*auren and I dated throughout April and May. By June we were inseparable. She'd finish my sentences and I'd finish hers. We held hands while walking and kissed whenever we said goodbye. Long walks through the park was not uncommon now. I'd visit her family and she'd visit mine. We were like Frick and Frack. We'd only miss seeing one another during work hours.

Lauren was still substitute teaching at various schools and looking for a permanent position. At every interview she went on in Bushwick, the principals wanted her to teach something other than music and Lauren was not about to compromise. She still had her job at the Blue Angel to quench her thirst for singing, though. Sometimes I'd sit in on a set at the Blue Angel and play my saxophone solo on Lauren songs. She loved whenever I did this because our performances fit so well together. I understood her and she understood me. We were becoming a team.

However, I would not commit to playing at the Blue Angel every weekend since I was helping Aunt Tabby plan her wedding, finding time to hang out with the guys, dating Lauren and going to church service on Sunday. Every now and then, I just needed some downtime to be still and listen to God's voice. Some Saturday nights, I'd listen to jazz after my shower and drift off to sleep. Kenny G's sax would lull me into resting peacefully on my couch.

On one date night, a cool breeze slipped through my front window while Lauren and I were relaxing on my living room couch. Lauren trembled and I asked her if she'd like a throw to cover herself as we watched a romantic comedy on television. She nodded yes with a grin that would light up Broadway on the darkest night. I quickly stepped into my room and found the throw my mom used to cover me up with as I'd fall asleep on the sofa. It was royal blue and as soft as a cloud. I told Lauren the story of the throw as I covered her with it. She felt even more cozy in it after what I'd just shared.

We laughed and cried as we ate popcorn and fruit while watching the movie. We were truly kindred spirits, and we were so comfortable with each other. We started to kiss. Her lips were like satin pressing against my skin. I wanted to live forever in her embrace. She smelt like a rose and her breath was cool and minty. I loved kissing Lauren. We had to end some of our dates early now because things were clearly becoming too intense in private cozy places like my apartment or in her living room at her dad's house. Yes, Lauren still lived at home due to her inability to get a full-time day job. However, we were both praying about that.

Lauren and I began only going out to restaurants, plays and to movie theaters after a while. We didn't want to be tempted to make our vows to God as Christians ineffective. We didn't want to give a fire a place to start. After all, we were two fine young African-American people who had a lot going for us. We were great friends with a lot in common, too. We could belly laugh together or cry together. This just proved to me more and more each day that God was looking out for me. He knew just what I needed it. Tasha was not meant for me.

Chapter 19

WEDDING DAY

School ended on the 28th of June and June 31st, my aunts wedding day, was fast approaching. My grandmother had arrived just a week ago. I was elated to see her and my Uncle Obie after almost 2 years. They joked that I had become a city boy and wanted to know when I would be coming back down south for a long visit. It was clear they missed Aunt Tabby and I, but they were not interested in relocating to New York.

It was also clear to me that they were getting older and slower as the years went by. They would need someone to help care for them soon. However, they would never want to burden others with their problems. Grandma's hair was completely gray now. It was that beautiful, almost white gray that recalls wonder years spent well and her skin was like caramel, smooth and glowing. Uncle Obie was his spicy old self, telling dated jokes that made everyone fall out of their seats with laughter. He was tall and dark, and still had all his teeth. Both loved Lauren and highly approved of me dating her. They were happy to see me happy. They were also happy for Aunt Tabby and Uncle Jordan. Grandma and Uncle Obie kept saying they would not have missed this wedding for anything in this world.

Grandma cooked for the entire week. The aroma of southern fried chicken, macaroni and cheese, and collard greens filled the air in our entire building. We all enjoyed that southern cuisine immensely. My stomach was so full, I thought I'd burst. Mrs. Sarah Mae Davis' food was filled with so much love and the history of our family's recipes having been passed down from generation to generation. She talked about putting sugar in the collard greens so they wouldn't taste bitter, and putting nutmeg and vanilla into her sweet potato pies. When I saw her passing this information on to Lauren, I knew she was trying to make Lauren a part of our family tree, too. Grandma never shared those recipes with anyone outside of our family. Those were her secret recipes. Lauren was eager to please my family members and accepted the challenge of possibly becoming a part of our family one day.

Finally, the day was here: June 31st Aunt Tabitha's wedding day. Aunt Tabitha was about to marry the man of her dreams. It had been a long journey to get to this point. You see, during Aunt Tabby's three year relationship with Jordan they found out Aunt Tabby could not conceive children. Initially, she thought no man would be interested in having a long-term relationship with a woman who could never have a child, but Jordan loved my aunt in spite of that. Both wanted children, but loved each other more than their infertility situation. Tabby was now 40 years old and enjoyed working with children daily as a school nurse. She could not understand why some of the students she cared for had parents who abused their children, while she and Uncle Jordan wanted children so badly and had none. During her 10 year career, Aunt Tabby reported several of these parents in order to get these poor children out of their dire situations.

I felt it was sad those parents were allowed to have kids when Tabby and Jordan couldn't. But who was I to question God. I thought to myself, *Maybe someday they'll adopt a child.* Now that marriage was on the table, the next natural step for most couples would surely be having or adopting children. Jordan, and Tabitha would be amazing parents for a child.

The church was full, bright, and beautifully decorated. There were white orchids everywhere. It smelled like a spring garden. Silence fell across the sanctuary as my aunt walked down the aisle to my future Uncle Jordan. Uncle Obie and Tabitha floated slowly down the aisle to the pianist's rendition of "Here Comes the Bride." Aunt Tabby looked angelic in her floral, embroidered, white lace gown. She smiled so widely, you saw all of her gleaming white teeth. She was ready.

Jordan beamed with pride as he stood transfixed in her glow. He wore a traditional black tuxedo with tails as he held out his hand to her as she approached the altar. Pastor Larry Wilson, Lauren's father, had to remind Jordan not to kiss Tabby until the end of the ceremony. Everyone laughed politely at his reminder. I stood beside Jordan as his best man about to cry huge tears of joy when passing him the wedding ring to place on my aunt's finger.

Grandma balled like a baby. When they pronounced Uncle Jordan and Aunt Tabitha man and wife the usher had to bring grandma a whole box of tissues. Those were happy tears, because her youngest daughter had finally found happiness and was getting married. They had to redo my grandmother's makeup in order to take the wedding pictures, but by the time we arrived at the Blue Angel for the reception everyone was ready to celebrate. Food, great conversation, music and love were shared by family and friends throughout the evening. I'll remember that day forever.

Chapter 20

DAVID'S SONG

One month later, my neighborhood is thriving. Asia is not only attending church with us, but she has decided to give her heart to the Lord. Asia has also completed her GED program in record time. She is getting a part time job while applying to nursing school. Praise God! Asia's grandmother is so proud of her granddaughter, now. I can't wait to see what God has in store for her next. Guess what? Asia's landlord didn't sell the building and Asia's new job will help to pay rent. The landlord has delayed the rent increase for all the tenants who catch up on their current rent payments. He saves money by not going to court to evict those tenants. So, Asia is smiling everyday now.

Aunt Tabby and Uncle Jordan have just found out that they are expecting their own little bundle of joy. Yes, God performed a miracle and my aunt is pregnant with her first child. Of course, yours truly will be the baby's godfather and first cousin. So, we are expecting a visit from grandma Mae and Uncle Obie again soon. Also, Tabby and Jordan are closing on their three story-high brownstone in two weeks. This means we will be moving about five blocks away in a few days.

As for me, David Reed, I stopped by the Blue Angel last night to surprise my girl, Lauren. I played sax for her set, but at the end I had my own little surprise planned. You see, I popped the question after playing a new piece I'd written called David's Song. It is about my love for the Lord and my love for Lauren. Lauren was in tears by the end of the song and that's when I bent down on one knee to ask for her hand in marriage. To my surprise, she said yes. So you see, "All things work together for good!" I guess you could say, for now, I've found my song.

TO MY READERS

Thanks so much for reading my book. I hope you enjoyed it.

If you would like to submit a review of my books on Amazon, or other places where my books are sold feel free to do so at the following places online.

www.amazon.com

teresawhitakersbooks.wordpress.com

teesblog.video.blog

Sincerely,

Teresa Whitaker

teestalktime1@gmail.com

ABOUT THE AUTHOR

Teresa Whitaker is a retired New York City public school teacher with a lifelong love of storytelling and connection. Now a blogger, podcast host, and app developer, she brings heart, humor, and a touch of hope to everything she creates. Her debut romance novel, *Neighbor Needed: Only the Exceptional Need Apply*, introduced readers to a world of unexpected love in a community on the brink of change. Her sequel, *Neighbor Needed 2: David's Song*, continues that journey with even deeper emotion. Teresa lives in Brooklyn, New York, where love stories unfold every day—both on and off the page.

www.ingramcontent.com/pod-product-compliance
Lightning Source LLC
Chambersburg PA
CBHW061138200626
46817CB00016B/1976